3.99

This book is to be returned on or before

AUTHOR Story books

TITLE Polly Thumb

Date	
. . . .	. . . .
. . . .	. . . .
. . . .	. . . .
. . . .	. . . .
. . . .	. . . .
. . . .	. . . .

For David, with love – H.C.

For Clare – P.K.

First published in Great Britain in 1994
by Simon & Schuster Young Books
Campus 400
Maylands Avenue
Hemel Hempstead
Herts HP2 7EZ

Typeset in 16/25 Bembo by Goodfellow & Egan Ltd, Cambridge
Printed and bound in Portugal by Edicoes ASA

British Library Cataloguing in Publication Data available

ISBN 0 7500 1548 9
ISBN 0 7500 1549 7 (pbk)

Helen Cresswell

Polly Thumb

Illustrated by Peter Kavanagh

SIMON & SCHUSTER
YOUNG BOOKS

Chapter One

I bet you don't believe in magic. I bet you
don't believe in dragons and magic lamps and
wishes. I didn't. What – magic, on our street?
On yours? You must be joking.

    You had better watch out.

My name is Polly Dawkins and I live at
number eight Victoria Road. My brother
Sam is two years older than me, and thinks
he's the bee's knees. (Do bees *have* knees?) We
both go to Witherspoon Road Primary School.

Our Mum and Dad go out to work, and
we have a dopey dog called Pineapple. I
know that's a silly name for a dog, but don't
blame me. My mum picked it. If you ask me,
the reason why he's so dopey is because he's
got a dopey name. If *my* name were
Pineapple, I think I'd be dopey.

Here's how the magic happened. It was the school holidays. We have to have someone to look after us while Mum and Dad are at work. This year, it was this student called Wendy.

She was a real pain. She didn't like us and we didn't like her. One day she deliberately broke up my thousand piece jigsaw, when I'd slotted in at least nine hundred and fifty three pieces. I told her she'd done it on purpose.

"So what?" she said.

"I don't like you," I told her.

"And I don't like *you*, or your rotten brother. I'm only doing it for the money."

That's how horrible she was. She only let us have three fish fingers instead of four, and she had *six* herself! And she never took us anywhere, even though Mum had said we could go swimming, or to the ice rink. Most of the time she painted her finger and toe nails a horrible red, and watched television. We were always plotting ways to get rid of her.

This particular day we were in the garden. I've got my own patch, and I was sowing parsley. When it came up, I was going to charge Mum ten pence a bunch. I'm saving up for a skate board.

Sam just stood throwing stones at a rusty old bucket. It was upside down over Dad's rhubarb.

Clunk! Clunk!

The stones kept hitting the bucket. It began to get on my nerves.

"Pity you haven't got any brains," I said.

"What d'you mean?
I've got more brains than…"

"People with brains don't
spend all day just
chucking stones at buckets."

"You shut up!"

He was holding a stone ready to chuck, and
for a minute I thought he was going to throw
it at me.

"I just wish you'd go away,"
I said.

"And I wish *you* would,"
said Sam.

"I just wish you'd shrink
and shrivel and… oh crumbs!"

"Help!" I screamed.

I didn't know what was happening.

All at once the ground was coming up to meet me with a rush. And at the same time the world was getting bigger and BIGGER and *BIGGER*!

"I didn't mean it! Stop!" shouted Sam.

Chapter Two

Whatever it was that was happening, stopped happening. The world stood still again. The only trouble was, the world was fifty times bigger than it had been.

I seemed to be standing on the moon. All round me were brown humps and hollows. Not far off I could see something metal glinting in the sun.

"It must be my space craft," I thought. (It wasn't. It was the garden trowel.)

I was just looking round, and deciding I couldn't be on the moon, because there was so much green, when – THUD!

Something enormous came plonking down right by me. I screamed, but it didn't come out as a scream. It was just a squeak.

Whatever it was was a kind of dirty
white, with a long rope trailing down.

THUD!

Now there was another of them.
I squeaked again.

"Polly! Polly, are you all right?"

It was Sam's voice. That was funny.
The voice seemed to be coming from
somewhere in the sky. I looked up
and saw two long blue pillars.
Then there was a huge red splodge.
It was a really bright red,
just like Sam's anorak.

Suddenly, the blue pillars just folded in half
as if they were on hinges. The red came
rushing down towards me. I looked round
for cover, and found it. A whole lot of green
umbrellas on one stick. I ran and crouched
under them. I shut my eyes.

This can't be a nightmare, I thought,
or I'd be *opening* my eyes, not shutting them.

"Polly!"

It was Sam's voice, again, very loud.
I opened my eyes. Right in front of me was
a pair of huge, enormous eyes. They were
fringed with eyelashes like bicycle spokes.

"I don't believe it!"

That was when I saw the mouth. It was
a red cave with teeth the size of tombstones.

I clung on tightly to the umbrella tree.

"Sam!" I squeaked. "Help! Giant!"

"I *am* Sam, idiot!"

"Well, *do* something!"

WHOOSH! I was flying through the air again – upwards this time. I wriggled and kicked, but two soft pink pincers held me tightly.

Then I was free. I looked round and saw that I was standing on an enormous, lumpy pink cushion. A *dirty*, lumpy pink cushion. It seemed to be moving. I tottered to the edge and looked over.

16

"Help!" I squeaked. The ground was miles away below. I can't stand heights. I was so dizzy that I shut my eyes again and sat down.

"I don't believe it!" said Sam's voice. "Like Tom Thumb! *Polly* Thumb!"

I opened my eyes. There were these eyes again. This time, I did recognize them. And I realized that the dirty pink cushion was the palm of Sam's hand.

This is me, Polly Dawkins, I told myself. I'm Polly Dawkins and I'm eight years old and I don't believe in magic. And I'm sitting in my own brother's hand. Better just give it a nip, in case we're both dreaming.

I leaned forward and bit one of his fingers, as hard as I could.

"Owch!" he yelped, "Look out – or I'll drop you!"

I sat there trying to work things out. One
minute I had been sowing parsley, the next
I had shrunk. Why hadn't Sam shrunk?
I tried to think back. Then I remembered.

"It's *you*!" I said. "It's your fault, it's all
your fault!"

"I know." He sounded so miserable that I almost felt sorry for him.

"Go on then – wish me back again."

"But I don't know *how*! I'm always wishing things, and they never happen."

"Well, they have this time," I told him. "Worse luck for me. Go on – wish me back."

"I'd feel silly."

"How do you think *I* feel? And what do you think Mum and Dad will say when they get home?"

That did it. He took a deep breath that sounded like the wind in the chimney.

"I wish — "

"Stop!" I yelled.

"But I thought you said — "

"Not yet! I'm in your hand!"

I had this picture of me, normal size,
balancing on one leg in the palm of Sam's
hand. I giggled. I knew it wasn't really funny,
but I giggled anyway.

"Put me down first, idiot."

The fat pink sausages went round me again, and next minute I was back on the moon, among the umbrella trees.

"Now do it."

"I wish you'd go back to your normal size!"

I waited for the sky to come rushing down to meet me.

"Please!" he added.

Nothing. He said it again, then again. Nothing.

"Polly! Sam!"

"Quick – it's Wendy!"

Things happened fast. The next thing
I knew I was in a deep dark dungeon. A soft,
warm dungeon. I was in Sam's pocket.

"Dinner time!"

I heard Sam groan.

"That's torn it!" he said.

It was all right for him. Have *you* ever been
in your brother's pocket, among all the
crushed-up crisps and half-sucked sweets?
It was sausages for dinner, I knew that.

"Where's Polly?"

"Hiding in the shed," Sam said. "Says she
doesn't want any dinner."

What a fib! I kicked him, hard.

"That's all right by me," I heard Wendy say. "All the more for us."

"I want sausages, I want sausages!" I yelled.

Next minute I was whisked out and plonked back on the ground.

"Shut up! She'll hear you!"

"Who cares?
I want sausages!"

"I'll save you some. I'll bring you some out."

His dirty great trainers went kicking off.

Now what?

I'll tell you what. The next thing I knew
I was being prodded by something hard and
yellow. A blackbird had mistaken me for a
worm. (Cheek!)

"Get off, get off!"
I waved my arms and
yelled. The blackbird
spread its enormous
wings and took off.

That was a close shave. Here I was wanting *my* dinner, and I nearly ended up as a blackbird's dinner. Next time, I might not be so lucky. I ran and took shelter under a tree – a rose bush, I mean.

There, I had a good think. Why had Sam's wish come true? When he made it, he had been throwing stones at a bucket. I'd read about magic stones in stories. I had never believed them. Now, I was not so sure.

I felt very lost and very lonely. In fact, I may as well tell you, I started to cry.

Chapter Four

Snuff! Snuffle snuffle! Something cold and damp was nudging my legs. There above me was a mountain of fur.

"Pineapple!"

A long pink tongue came out. It was nearly as big as I was. Lick, lick! It nearly knocked me over.

"Oh Pineapple!" I sobbed. "At least *you* know me!"

I expect he knew me by my smell. (Not
that I think I'm smelly, it's just that dogs have
very sharp noses.)

"Good old Pineapple! When I come right
again, I'm going to give you the biggest bone
in the world!"

He wagged his tail and padded off into the house. I expect he could smell sausages.

I decided that I would go into the house, too. Why not? Nobody would see me. I was getting hungrier and hungrier.

The house seemed a very long way off. What if that blackbird saw me? I tugged a leaf from a plant and held it over my head, as camouflage. Then I set off.

At last I reached the back door, and saw to my relief that Sam had left it partly open. I dropped my leaf. That was when I saw him.

Tiger, next door's cat, was streaking towards me over the grass. I have never moved so fast in my life. I shot into the kitchen. Luckily, one of the cupboard doors was open. I ran inside it and tried to push the door shut, but it was too heavy.

I was in the cupboard where Mum keeps saucepans and baking tins. I ran behind the nearest saucepan and peered out.

There was Tiger with his huge eyes. Usually, I like him. I give him saucers of milk when Pineapple isn't looking. Now, he was my enemy. He wanted to catch me and eat me.

"It's only me," I said.

He dabbed a paw inside the cupboard and I shot back behind the saucepan. There was a landslide of pans and tins. They all spilled out of the cupboard with a clatter.

I screamed and dodged out of the way. Tiger streaked half way across the kitchen and stood glaring and hissing.

Then he shot off as Pineapple went chasing after him.

"Who's made all that mess?" It was Wendy's voice.

"Must've been the cat. Probably saw a mouse."

Mouse? MOUSE? First I'd been taken for a worm, now a mouse. I stayed behind my saucepan and held my breath.

"You'd better clear it up," Wendy said.

"But we haven't had pudding!"

"There isn't any."

"But Mum said there was some leftover chocolate mousse!"

"I've eaten it," Wendy said.

Talk about greedy.

"Put those things back in the cupboard and do the washing up," she ordered Sam. "There's something I want to see on telly."

She went out. Sam's huge trainers came towards me. I ran out from behind the saucepan and waved my arms. I'd escaped from a blackbird and a cat. I didn't want to end up being squashed flat as a pancake.

"Sam! Sam!"

He knelt down.

"Tiger nearly got me!"

"Serve you right. What if *she'd* seen you?"

"She'd have had a fit!" I giggled. "Where's my sausage?"

"Sorry. She ate yours."

"Pig!"

"You go back in the garden while I wash up. I'll bring you a biscuit."

"It's *miles*!" I wailed. "And there are killer blackbirds out there! And killer cats!"

WHOOSH! Sam picked me up. He went into the garden and put me inside the rhubarb bucket.

"You'll be safe here. Shan't be long."

"And don't forget the biscuit!" I yelled after him.

Chapter Five

Sam brought me three chocolate digestives.
They were bigger than I was.

"You'll never eat all these," he said. "You
won't even eat one."

He broke one in small pieces and scoffed
the other two himself.

"I've been thinking
while I've been
sitting under
this bucket,"
I told him.

"What?"

"I've thought of a way to get rid of Wendy!"

36

"Wish we could," he said gloomily.

"When she came into the kitchen, I hid.
I thought she'd have a fit if she saw me."

"She'd have a fit, all right. A blue fit."

"So we *let* her see me!"

"What?"

"She'll think she's going mad!
It's *impossible*, me being this size."

"That's true."

"And if... and if..." Now for the really
brilliant bit. "If she saw me riding on
Pineapple's back, she'd have *ten* blue fits!"

Sam stared at me.

"Your brains can't be very big at the
moment," he said. "But you're a genius!"

"Yippee!" I could hardly wait.

"Pineapple!" Sam called. "Here, boy!"

Pineapple came padding over and stood
wagging his tail.

"You'll have to lift me on to his back,"
I told Sam. So he did. There I sat, clutching
Pineapple's long, thick fur. It was brilliant.
I seemed so far off the ground that it was like
being on an elephant – a furry elephant.

"What's it feel like?" asked Sam. You could
tell he was jealous.

"It's all warm and furry. Gee up!"

And we were off. I just couldn't believe it –
me, Polly Dawkins, riding a dog! I wanted
the whole world to see me.

Into the house we went, past the chair and
table legs in the kitchen, and up to the living
room door. Wendy was watching television,
as per usual. Sam whispered "Go for it, Poll!"
and pushed the door open.

Wendy was lying on the sofa, scoffing chocolate biscuits. You'd think she'd bust.

"Got a little surprise for you," said Sam. "And I mean little."

"Go away!" she said. "I'm busy."

Pineapple trotted forward. He can smell chocolate a mile off.

"Give him a biscuit," Sam said. "Mum always does."

"Get that smelly dog out of here!" snapped Wendy.

"He's *not* smelly!" I shouted. My voice had shrunk along with the rest of me, but by now we had reached the sofa and she must have heard it. "*You're* the one that's smelly!"

40

She turned then, and looked straight at me. I looked straight back and grinned. Then I stuck my tongue out. I've heard of people's eyes nearly popping out of their heads, but I'd never seen it before. Hers did. I honestly wouldn't have been surprised if they'd popped right out and on to the carpet – plop!

I gave her a wave.

That did it. She let out a scream, grabbed her bag, and ran. We heard the door bang after her.

"Hurray!" yelled Sam. "Good old Poll!"

"Now all you've got to do is to unwish that wish," I told him. "You'd better start sorting through those stones. One of them must be magic."

I rode Pineapple all the way back to the rhubarb bucket. There was quite a heap of stones lying where Sam had chucked them.

"It must have been one of them," I said. "You'd better get started. I'm off for a ride. Have a nice time!"

Sam picked up a stone. I heard him say "I wish Polly was the right size again!" Nothing happened. He was going to have a very boring afternoon.

Not me. I was making the most of riding my own dog.

I tried to get Pineapple to go the way I
wanted. I tried tweaking his left ear for left
and his right for right, but it didn't work.
I told you he was dopey.

Then I had a brilliant idea.

"Sam, fetch the camera!" I shouted.
"Then you can . . ."

All of a sudden my feet hit the ground and
Pineapple shot away from under me.

"Bingo!" I shouted. I stood swaying,
dizzy, but normal size again.

Sam came towards me, holding a stone. We both gazed at it, and we were both thinking the same thing. It looked like a perfectly ordinary brown stone, but . . .

"I wish – I wish I had a brand new bike like Joe Bailey's!"

Nothing.

"Please," added Sam.

Nothing.

"So that's that," I said. "Pity. But at least we've got rid of Wendy!"

"But what are we going to tell Mum and Dad?"

"The truth," I said. "Don't worry – they'll never believe us."

They didn't, either. They just said Wendy was too unreliable, and found someone else to look after us. And *she* takes us to the ice rink, and the swimming pool. *And* she lets us have four fish fingers each.

RULES FOR
My Room
1. No Siniging.
2. No sitting on the bed.
3. No Taking my Toys with out Permmision
4. Knock before entering
5. No messing with magic.

So it all turned out well, in the end. Lucky for me. But remember – don't mess about with magic!

Look out for more titles in the Yellow Storybooks series:

The Excitement of Being Ernest by Dick King-Smith

The other dogs in Ernest's village aren't a very friendly bunch. There's a German Short-haired Pointer, a French Bulldog, a Finnish Spitz and even a Tibetan Terrior. They all look down their well-bred noses at poor Ernest, who doesn't even know what *kind* of dog he is!

The Twenty Ton Chocolate Mountain by Helen Muir

Mr McWeedie doesn't teach the children much about reading or adding up. Instead, he tells them about spaghetti trees and singing sunflowers – and the Twenty Ton Chocolate Mountain.

Hurray for Monty Ray! by Sam McBratney

Monty Ray has a new baby brother – the sixth boy in the family! Nobody can think of a name for the new baby, so he's just called Lamb Chop. Monty Ray is very worried – what if the name sticks?

Beach Baby by Frances Usher

Belinda has always been a beach baby. Ever since she was born, she has loved to live by the sea. But one day her mother announces they will be moving to the town. How will Belinda cope so far away from her beloved beach?

Tall Tale Tom by Anne Forsyth

Tom is an ordinary black-and-white cat with an extraordinary talent for making up tall tales. His fibs always land him in trouble, until the day that he find himself the hero of the whole town!

Storybooks can be bought from your local bookshop or can be ordered direct from the publishers. For more information, write to: *The Sales Department, Simon & Schuster Young Books, Campus 400, Maylands Avenue, Hemel Hempstead HP2 7EZ.*